Racing with the Sun

McGraw Hill SRA

Columbus, OH

SRAonline.com

 SRA

ISBN: 978-0-07-608746-4
MHID: 0-07-608746-8

1 2 3 4 5 6 7 8 9 NOR 13 12 11 10 09 08 07

The *McGraw-Hill* Companies

I hate to admit it, but sometimes when I'm in science class my mind starts to wander. When the sun comes through the windows, it warms the classroom to the perfect temperature for daydreaming. Today though I was paying attention because Mrs. Barrett was explaining how some scientists explore ways to make fuel for cars out of garbage. That would be good, I was thinking, because at our house we make a lot of garbage. I know because it's my job to take it out.

Well maybe I *was* daydreaming a little, because suddenly Mrs. Barrett was calling on me to answer a question. "Marcus? Marcus!"

"Um," I said, "can you repeat the question?"

"Identify three renewable energy sources."

"Wind energy is renewable. And I guess garbage is pretty renewable too," I said.

My friend Jerry, who sits behind me, laughed.

"Garbage *is* renewable, if you think about it," Mrs. Barrett laughed. "I can't imagine fast-food restaurants ever running out of cooking oil, so I think we'll have the ingredients for biodiesel—a cleaner fuel made from renewable sources—for a long time. Can you think of one more?"

I thought about the sun shining through the windows and heating up the room. "Sun energy!" I said.

"Yes, sun energy—or solar energy—is an important renewable resource," said Mrs. Barrett.

Jerry spoke up. "It seems like there would be lots of problems using solar energy or wind energy, though. I mean the sun doesn't shine everywhere all the time, and the wind isn't a reliable energy source either."

"That's true," said Mrs. Barrett. "But scientists are working on those problems, and the technology is becoming easier and cheaper to use."

When I got home from school my sister Alexis was already there, stuffing shirts into the washing machine. She lives in a dormitory at college, but she visits every few days to do laundry and have dinner with us.

"Hey, Lex," I said, tossing my backpack into the closet and kicking off my shoes.

Later, as we sat down for dinner, Alexis asked us if we'd ever heard of the North American Solar Challenge. Mom and Dad looked at her like they didn't know what she was talking about. "It's a race. Actually, it's a R-A-Y-C-E," she said, laughing as if she had told a hilarious joke. "They use the sun's *rays* to *race* cars," she said. "Teams compete to design the best solar car and drive it across the country—2,500 miles!"

"That does sound like quite a challenge!" said Dad.

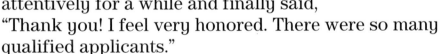

Mom looked carefully at Alexis. "So . . . why are you telling us this?"

"Well," said Alexis, "I applied to be on the team."

At that moment the phone rang and Alexis jumped up saying, "That's probably for me. Keep your fingers crossed!" She cleared her throat, picked up the phone, and said "Hello?" in a voice that was very serious and not at all like her normal voice. She listened attentively for a while and finally said, "Thank you! I feel very honored. There were so many qualified applicants."

As she hung up I noticed that I'd been holding my breath. I let it out in a loud *whoosh* while Mom and Dad stood up and hugged Alexis until she gasped.

"Congratulations!" said Mom.

"I'm so excited!" Alexis yelled. "I made it even though it was really competitive. You wouldn't believe how many other students applied!"

"You know, Lex," I said, "we were just talking about solar energy in school today. Mrs. Barrett said that more energy reaches Earth than we could ever use. We just need to find ways to collect it."

"Well," said Alexis, "that's the point of the North American Solar Challenge. We're working on harnessing energy from the sun to power cars, but that energy can be used other places too, like in people's homes for heating and electricity."

"Maybe I could help somehow," I said.

"Yeah, that would be fun!" she said. "I wish I could think of a way . . . but you need to have a lot of experience to help design a solar car. I mean some of the team members have been studying engineering for years." I must have looked disappointed because she smiled and added, "If I think of anything, though, I'll be sure to tell you."

I stayed after science class the next day because I was bursting to tell Mrs. Barrett the exciting news about Alexis. "Guess what! My sister Alexis is on the solar car team for her college. They're going to compete in the North American Solar Challenge!"

"That's excellent, Marcus!" said Mrs. Barrett. "I remember when Alexis was in my class. She was a top student. Did you know there are solar car competitions for middle school students, too, called Junior Solar Sprints?"

"How can there be when we can't even drive yet?" I asked.

"These races are for model solar cars," said Mrs. Barrett. "Teams of students from middle schools all over the country design and build model solar cars and race them. The races are sponsored by the National Renewable Energy Laboratory, but different schools around the county host the events. Here, take a look at this brochure about the races."

"I might be interested in doing something like that," I said. "I'm starting to think that researching ways to use renewable energy instead of fossil fuels like coal is really important. I never thought about it seriously before. Does our school have a team?"

"No. At least, not yet," Mrs. Barrett answered. "If we work together, we might get enough people interested to form a team."

I thought about that for a minute. "Maybe if I write an article about the North American Solar Challenge for the school paper, I could get people interested in solar power," I said.

"That's a great idea!" Mrs. Barrett said. "In fact, maybe you could use your sister as a source for your article. You could write it as an insider's view of the race. I think that would get people to take notice. In the meantime I'll ask Principal Ramos what he thinks about forming a team."

Several weeks later, Alexis stopped by for dinner.

"How is the solar car coming?" I asked.

She picked at her pizza, mumbling something about how it was hard work but it was fun. Somehow she didn't seem as enthusiastic as I expected.

"Have you had any problems with the car design?" asked Mom.

"No," said Alexis. "The car is amazing. It'll be efficient and fast and will even look great. I've been working on the chassis—that's the frame or the skeleton of the car. We've made it out of materials light enough so that it won't take a lot of energy to move the car, but also sturdy enough that the wind isn't going to push it all over the road. Everything is on schedule. The only problem is that we can't think of a good name for the car!"

I had never considered it before, but I suppose each team had to come up with a cool name for their car. "What about *Solstice*, as in 'Summer Solstice'?" I asked.

"Another team is already using that name," Alexis said. "And we can't use anything with *Raycer* in it, because that's taken too."

We sat in silence for a few minutes, thinking about possible names. "Speaking of solar cars," I said, "I decided to write an article on the North American Solar Challenge for the school newspaper."

"Really?" said Alexis. "Do you want to come with me to our team's headquarters for a firsthand look at the car? We're starting to assemble it, so maybe we could even give you a demonstration."

Mom and Dad nodded that I could go, and we agreed that Alexis would pick me up the following Saturday.

Early Saturday morning, Alexis and I headed to campus to visit the solar car team's headquarters. Marie, the team leader, and Leo, another team member, were already there, working on the car.

"Hey, you two," said Alexis. "My brother is writing an article about the race for his school newspaper, so I thought he should come along and have a look at what goes on behind the scenes."

Leo offered to give me a tour of the solar car. "I wish we could give you a demonstration of how it all works, but we've got some work to do on the battery pack before we can take a test drive."

"The battery pack?" I asked.

"The battery pack is similar to the gas tank in a gasoline-powered car. It stores some of the solar energy that has been collected," Leo explained.

I wrote *Battery pack stores energy like a gas tank* in my notebook while Leo continued.

"We have a new type of battery this year, made out of lithium," he said. "Lithium batteries are lighter than the old lead-acid batteries, but the technology is more recent. We'll have to watch them carefully to make sure they work properly."

Leo pointed to the top of the car. "This is the solar array. It's made of photovoltaic solar cells, the same kind they use on satellites. Each solar cell converts energy from the sun into electrical energy."

I wrote *Photovoltaic* in my notebook after asking Leo how to spell it. Then I had a sudden inspiration. "I just thought of a great name for your car. What about *Photo Finish*? You know, when a car wins a close race, sometimes people call it a 'photo finish.'"

Leo nodded thoughtfully and then grinned.

After months and months of waiting, the day of the race finally came. Dad and I drove all the way to Texas to see it begin. The weather was clear and sunny, and the crowd was cheering. Leo was just strapping himself into the flat-topped solar car, which had been painted orange and was nearly covered with the huge solar array. I squinted to read what was written on the side of the car: *Photo Finish.* "Dad, look!" I said. "They decided to use the name I thought of!"

"So you were able to help out after all, Marcus," said Dad, smiling.

"Leo told me that each car's battery pack is fully charged when they start the race," I explained. "After that, they can only use energy they collect from the sun through the solar array."

Just then the announcer shouted, "And they're off!"

Everyone cheered, especially Dad and me.

Dad and I met Alexis and her team after the day's drive was complete. The first leg of the race had gone well, and almost all of the cars had made it to the first stop without any big problems. Alexis described the team's strategy. "As long as it's sunny and clear, we cruise along at highway speeds," she said. "We need to keep the batteries charged though, in case we drive into rain or an area with dense clouds."

"Tomorrow we start the second leg which is one thousand miles long," Leo explained. "We'll go as far as we can each day in ten hours. That's when you'll see whose design is the most efficient and whose strategy is working."

As we left, we reminded Alexis to call us with periodic updates since we could not follow the team for the entire race.

Alexis called at the end of the fifth day to tell us how the race was going. "We're in first place, and our team's strategy is working perfectly. We're trying to conserve battery power by going at a steady pace, but some teams race at full speed, hoping to stay ahead of bad weather."

She explained that in the morning there had been light rain and cloudy skies. Several of the teams, hoping to drive out of the rain and into clear conditions, began the day at top speeds. Then they ran into some severe thunderstorms and had to pull over and wait for the rain to pass.

"It was raining so hard that they couldn't even see," she said. "Some of the cars' batteries died and the teams had to recharge them, which takes a long time in the rain."

"We went more slowly to conserve battery power, and by the time we got there the worst of the rain had passed," Alexis explained. "We saw three or four cars pulled over at the side of the road. After we passed the leading team's car, we whooped it up. We were in first place!"

After I passed the phone to Mom, I decided to work on my article. I wanted to make sure I had all the details of the race just right so that other kids in my school would be inspired to start a solar car team for the Junior Solar Sprint. I'd even thought of a good title for my article: *Solar Raycing—Not Just for Fun.* The race would be fun, of course, but the science behind it was very important. Someday we all might be able to use that solar energy for electricity instead of burning coal and petroleum products.

Three more days went by before we heard from Alexis again, and this time she reported some bad news.

"We had some trouble, but we think we can still finish the race," she said. "We drove straight into a thunderstorm today with pouring rain and hail the size of ping-pong balls. Before we could pull over and cover up the car, twenty of the solar cells had been damaged. It took hours to repair the array."

"Are you still in first place?" I asked, hoping the other cars had been slowed down by the storm.

"Right now we're in fourth place," Alexis said. "Three other cars passed us while we were making repairs, since they were far enough behind that they missed the storm altogether. It was unfortunate for us, but we're trying to stay optimistic."

Then Alexis changed the subject. "I have some good news too," she said brightly. "One of the big sports networks is covering the last three days of the race. That means you might be able to see us on television!"

After we hung up, I turned on channel 74 to see if they were showing the North American Solar Challenge. I was hoping to get a glimpse of *Photo Finish* or even Alexis and the other team members in the lead and chase vehicles. Those were the cars that carried all the team members except Leo, who was driving the solar car.

I wasn't disappointed. We did see *Photo Finish*, and we even saw Leo give an interview to a reporter. "We're behind now because of some bad luck with the weather," he said, "but you can never tell what will happen tomorrow."

Over the next few days we were able to watch the race on television. We saw Alexis's team start out the morning after the big hailstorm looking excited and determined. The last of the storm systems had moved off to the east and the sun shone brightly through a few fluffy clouds. Toward the end of the day, the team that had been in second place took a wrong turn and ended up losing time when they tried to find the correct route again. Because of that mistake, Alexis's team was able to move into third place.

Late in the afternoon the car that had been leading by more than an hour drove over a huge pothole in the road. One of the wheels bent and the team had to pull to the side of the road to fix it.

As the last day of the race began, a cloudy sky and a sprinkle of rain forced the *Photo Finish* team to make a difficult decision. Should they drive as fast as possible and risk draining their battery before they were able to make it to a sunnier area? Or should they play it safe and conserve battery power in case of bad weather?

The announcer on the sports network said this was one of the closest solar races he'd ever seen. The car in first place, *Light Raycer,* had only a fifteen-mile lead over *Photo Finish.* It even looked like *Photo Finish* was closing the gap. When the clouds finally cleared though, *Light Raycer* was still ahead.

We watched as *Photo Finish* crossed the finish line minutes after *Light Raycer.* Then Leo jumped out and ran to hug the other team members.

Alexis came over to celebrate as soon as she got back into town. After the hugging was over and "Congratulations!" was said nearly a thousand times, I pulled out a copy of the morning newspaper.

"I have a surprise," I said. I opened the paper to the sports section. There, on the front page, was the headline *Solar Raycing—Not Just for Fun, by Marcus Hutchins.* A picture of Alexis's team standing by *Photo Finish* was printed next to my article.

Alexis grabbed the newspaper. She started reading out loud from my article. "Family and friends of the *Photo Finish* team members are proud to report that the team placed second in the North American Solar Challenge. The 2,500-mile race took ten days to complete. The only fuel used to power the cars was energy from the sun."

"I thought you wrote an article for your school newspaper!" Alexis said, surprised.

"I did write it for the school paper, but when your team did so well, the city newspaper decided to print it too. And after Principal Ramos read it, he agreed to let our school compete in the Junior Solar Sprint—the model solar car race—next year. Maybe I'll even be on the team." Then I added, "Keep reading. You're leaving out the most important part."

Alexis smiled as she read the end of the article: "Alexis Hutchins, one team member, said the experience was the most fun she's ever had. Even though team members had a great time building and racing a solar car, they didn't just do it for fun. They were proving that solar energy is a practical alternative to burning fossil fuels."

Vocabulary

reliable (ri lī´ ə bəl) (page 4) *adj.* Able to be depended on.

fossil fuels (fôs´ əl fyōō´ əls) (page 9) *n.* Plural of **fossil fuel:** A fuel formed from the remains of plants and animals. Coal and petroleum are fossil fuels.

demonstration (de´ mən strā´ shən) (page 11) *n.* Something that explains, proves, or shows something clearly.

converts (kən vûrts´) (page 13) A form of the verb **convert:** To change something into something different.

inspiration (in´ spə rā´ shən) (page 13) *n.* The stirring of the mind, feelings, or imagination, especially so that some good idea comes.

squinted (skwint´ əd) (page 14) *v.* Past tense of **squint:** To partially close the eyes.

charged (chärjd) (page 15) *v.* Past tense of **charge:** To fill with electricity.

severe (sə vir´) (page 16) *adj.* Very serious; dangerous.

Comprehension Focus: Author's Point of View

1. Is this story written in first-person point of view or third-person point of view? How can you tell?

2. In what point of view is Marcus's article written? Give an example of how you can tell.